The Sender Feels Better
series has been created to sow

seeds in children's hearts,

helping them find different

ways of coping with new

situations

Sender lives in a lovely town

With parks and forests and walks

People look out for each other
And neighbours stop to talk

Sender spends hours wandering around

Hunting out things he **likes**

From trees to sheep to dogs

From diggers to trucks to bikes

Sender's most favourite colour though

Is yellow so bright and shining

So whilst he's out wandering

Hunting out yellow never gets boring

Sender finds a *yellow petal*

So fragile and so soft

He pops it in his pocket

So it has no chance to get lost

Sender spots a yellow van

A grin spreads right across his face

Followed by a yellow cloud

This is such a special place!

Sender never thinks to say 'I'm bored'

Because wherever in the world he sits

If nothing comes to mind to do

Scanning his view for 'yellow' he picks

Sender's pal Eny, she loves **blue**

So whilst they hunt together

They look for different things to find
But it's not about who's better

Sender's other buddy Goo

He also loves to look

Goo though always looks for **red**

Red car, red shoe, red book

Sender likes that he and his friends

All like different shades

Even through the same window

They each find JOY from their own gaze

Sender uses this game sometimes

when he's got nowhere to go

Or if he's   or his friends are late
        lonely

He counts up all the yellow

Sender can sometimes feel a bit scared

If he's had a fright or **shock**

Something that always calms him down
Is wearing his yellow socks

Sender looks out of the window

There is rain and bins and smog

But he decides to only look

At the light yellow coloured dog

Sender thinks about his way

Of looking for what makes him happy

It's better than just seeing things

That leave him sad and feeling snappy

Sender, Goo and Eny meet

To go off on a new w....a....l.....k

Goo thinks he'll see a red crane

And Eny a dark blue rock

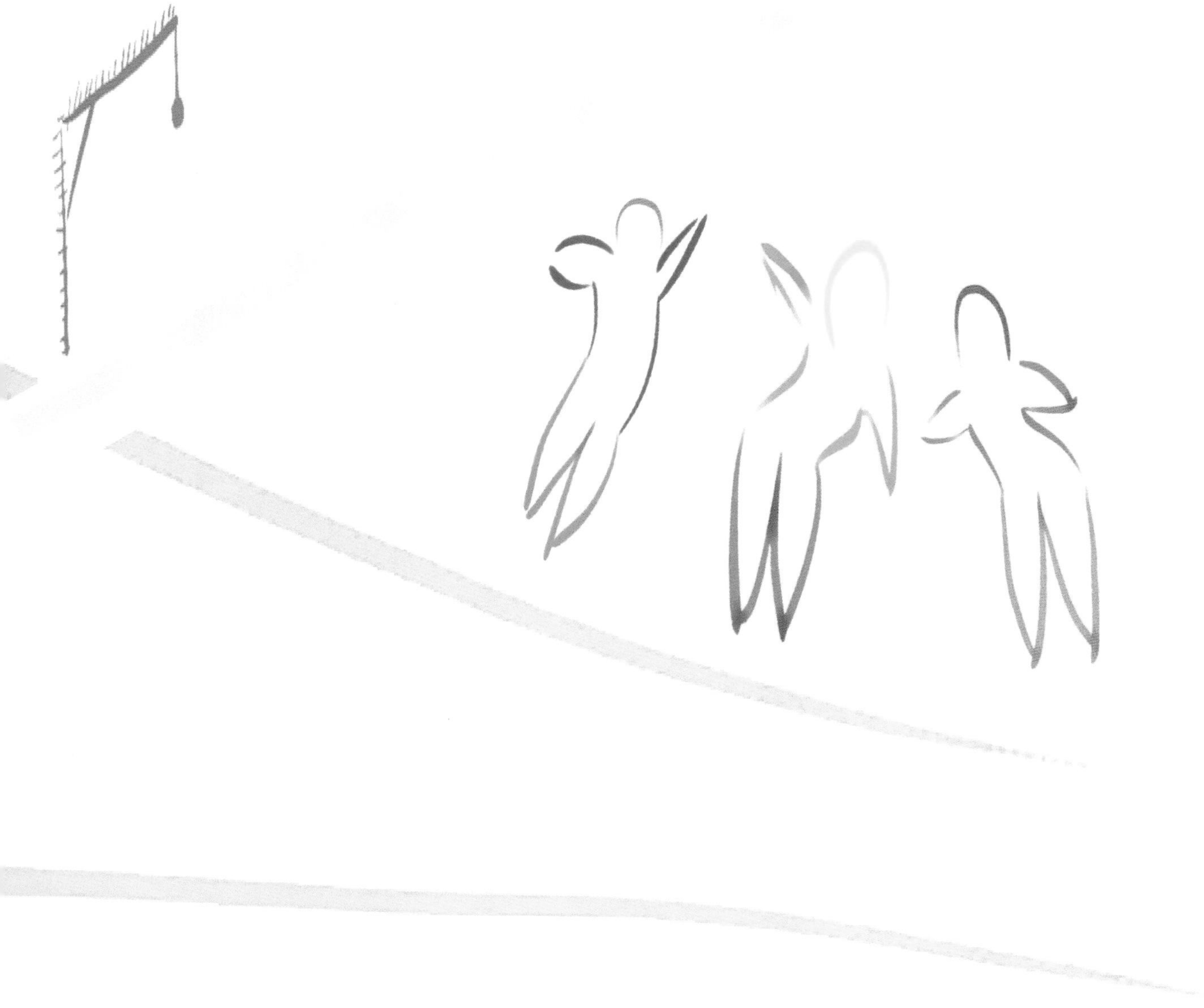

Sender sees a yellow coat

And Goo a red car wheel

Eny sees the bright blue sky

As they run laughing down the hill

Sender runs into his house
waving, heads straight on up to bed

He's had a really great day
With joy of yellow filling his head

Sender smiling snuggles into bed

Finds his petal and rests it down

It will be the first thing he sees when he wakes

He **loves** his little town

For Sebastian

Because even though there are days that are not filled with fun
You can find a feeling that makes you smile

Have you read Sender's Little Soldiers?

Look out for more books in the Sender Feels Better series!

Printed in Great Britain
by Amazon